THE INN OF
THE SEVEN STARS

KEVIN BECKETT

THE INN OF
THE SEVEN STARS

C AL CAME UPON the Inn of the Seven Stars at the crossroads when the sun was still high, casting chiaroscuro shadows through the branches of the old oaks crowding the road. Looking up at the sign held by rusty chains that screeched overhead, he stepped around hoofprints in the mud, which had filled with morning rainwater. The faded yellow paint on the flaking wood was indistinct, but Cal could see on it the seven stars that were the inn's namesake. The heavy door was half open to let in what sunlight there was.

Poking his head through the gap, what greeted him was the sight of a stout woman wiping down a large circular table. Other than her, the place seemed empty. His shadow blocked enough light that she looked up, revealing a round, tanned face of uncertain age and deep blue eyes. The few wisps of hair escaping her white kerchief were an equal mixture of auburn and grey.

"You here for a meal, or will you stay the night?"

Cal doffed his sagging brown hat, revealing a high pale brow and swept-back thin black hair that had receded from his scalp over the years. Eyebrows grew wild and black over his green eyes. A long aquiline nose peered over drooping mustachios, which would be less prominent if he didn't have several days of growth of white beard spread across his narrow face and coming to an angle at his pointed chin.

"I have silver enough for perhaps some bread and water, milady. Though if you trouble me for a song, I will give you more than its weight in gold."

Quickly, so as not to allow her to think too hard on what he said, long fingers unbuckled the pouch he carried with him, and he pulled out his prize. It was the key to a good night's rest in taverns such as these, or at least a key to someone's heart to feel enough pity to let him stay as a guest in some hut. It was his fiddle and bow.

"May I?"

The woman crossed thick arms across her chest, but she gave a slight nod, and Cal hoped his eyes were not fooling him that her thin-lipped mouth was twisting towards a hint of a smile.

He tucked the fiddle underneath his chin, with an initial bow scrape across the ridge to figure out the tuning. Nodding when it sounded right, he launched into a song, "To See My Love the Next Fair Morn". Stomping his boot to keep the rhythm, he began to sing in a high tenor that belied his age. He kept his eyes on her, only closing them during the plaintive chorus to accentuate the emotion.

As he opened his eyes, slowing the fiddle playing before letting one last note echo throughout the tavern, he was pleased to see one sandaled foot of hers tapping out the beat. Was there perhaps a light swaying of the hips? That would be encouraging.

"That's a nice song. I had never heard it before. Did you make it up yourself?"

"As flattering as that would be, no. It is a song by the Varesi, far east of here."

She cocked her head. "I do know where they are. Would occasionally get travelers staying at our old Inn, the Red Snake in Tarsunyal."

Cal could not conceal his grin. "I haven't been to that city since a dog's age. I remember my nights there quite fondly! What brings you to an inn out here?"

The woman raised an eyebrow. "Well, the war for one. The reavers of Scyral have been rattling their sabers again. With the rising tension, no one wanted just to come in and be merry. Those that did come wanted to drink too much. When word came that my aunt had died but left us with this, it seemed like a graceful way to exit the city. I'm too old to deal with yet another war for the kingdom's sake. Or empire or grand duchy, whatever they want to call it now."

Cal nodded. "It's why I keep to the backroads now," he said. "I'm not as quick with a blade as I used to be if they conscript again, and it was more luck than skill that kept me alive anyways. No, I earn my keep with this."

He motioned with his fiddle. The woman nodded, and he launched into another song. This time he did a little jig about the gondoliers of Bellardia. He glanced up, and the woman's shoulders were shifting to the music. Cal decided to end the song with a spiraling flourish of a solo that he closed his eyes to concentrate on. When he stopped, he was pleased to hear the sound of clapped hands.

"Ah, you know some Bellardians as well?"

"Oh, no. But that was a good song. I'm surprised. Every other minstrel in the city always auditioned with 'The Conquest of Love' or 'March towards Paradise.' Occasionally we would get someone who'd show off that they know 'Stand Tall Against the Dragon'. Then, when they played, it was all the usual chants, singalongs, and jigs to get the customers to join and become thirsty for another round. What you do is different."

Cal used the bow to tap his brow. "In this skull lies not just dozens, but hundreds of songs from all over the world."

"Most minstrels seem happy with a dozen or two."

"That is their right, but if all you get is the same dozen songs out of each of them, you do not get a good minstrel. They are all the same, no matter how good their voices and how talented they are on their instruments. If they are all the same, with nothing to set them apart, how can you truly tell which one is good and which one is bad?"

"Is that so? Does knowing too many songs make you a good minstrel then? All drunks want is songs they know."

"Ah, they say they do, but what they want in truth is to be part of something unique that music brings them. The drunks may not know the words yet, but they will feel the emotion the song gives them, and with that, they will remember their youth, of loves lost and warmth at home. They will remember good times they've had and bad ones they'd rather forget, and ..." Cal paused and looked knowingly at the woman. "Every emotion they feel will make them thirstier, and because they do not know the music in question, they will come back, not just for the minstrel, but for the emotions to be felt again and have another round."

The woman pulled out and sat on the chair beside the table she was cleaning. She beckoned Cal to sit opposite her, which he did.

"Alright, so what did you want? I can give you a bowl of stew and send you on your way if you need something for your belly. There's the town of Laurent a few hours west of here, so even if you tarry here a while, you'd still be there before nightfall." She stated that last word with a note of expectancy.

Cal leaned forward. "I have no doubt the stew's taste is warm and lovely, but I am hoping to leave here with silver and perhaps gold. What would it take to remain here for the night and entertain your customers?"

"Three sets of a dozen songs each. All throughout the night. No more than two ballads where everyone dies. This is a place for people to have a good time."

"I can fulfill those requirements. You mentioned stew. What about ale?"

"Hm, I would have figured you for a wine man. One draught of ale per set. No more nor less. You turn out to be a cheap drunk and can't perform, you get tossed outside, and some moss on the stones can be your pillow for the night."

"I assure you, I do know how to hold my liquor. Now, about that silver?"

"One per set, and you get paid at the end. You can sleep it off in one of the rooms upstairs. You get everyone singing and dancing by the second set, we'll throw in an extra silver, and I'll make breakfast of eggs and ham before we send you back out."

"Milady, I look forward to breakfast at your hands tomorrow." Cal shook her hand as callused in her own way as his own. "Calmondo Dezziardi," he said.

"Agwen of the Smiths."

With loud clumps from behind the bar, a trapdoor opened and a large bald man, whose face was anchored by a beard as black as night and shot through with grey, rose out of the opening. As his boots found purchase on the floor, Cal could see the man's height was taller than his own. A crooked nose suggested a past of it being broken and reset. Serpentine scars and sailor's tattoos raced along his massive forearms. The man carried a spade in one hand, coated with black earth.

"Well, there's nothing to be found but roots and more dirt. I swept the floor clean again ..." The man looked up and saw them at the table.

"Detmar, this is Calmondo," Agwen spoke first. "He's a minstrel who knows too many songs and wants to sing them tonight for a room and some silver. Calmondo, this is my husband. Any of the customers get to be a bother for you tonight, don't worry. He'll toss them out. If the customers decide you're too much of a bother, he'll toss you out."

"That won't be necessary, either of you. I know more than enough songs to please the audience, no matter who shows up."

Detmar looked at Cal with skepticism in his brown eyes. "That so? You know 'March Towards Paradise'?"

Agwen looked back at Calmondo with a twinkle in her eye. "Well, minstrel, do you? Perhaps you should do it for my husband here."

Suppressing a sigh, Cal pushed back the chair and stood up, and began to stomp out the rhythm to a song he had come to loathe.

• • •

After serving him a full meal of hot lamb stew and one ale, Agwen informed him it was on the house, for his recital of the song had pleased her husband.

Cal went to the cozy room with a ceiling just an inch too short for his head and cleaned himself from his travels. He shaved off the white stubble with a sharpened blade and some lathered soap, revealing a man who appeared ten years younger. After a hot bath, he changed into his minstrel's motley, doing his best to suck in the potbelly that had grown on his slender frame over the past few years. Taking his fiddle and bow, he walked down the stairs to see what his audience would be for the evening.

He'd initially been concerned, when having a bowl of stew while the sun was high, and the Inn deserted, that he would only play for the owners as his audience. However, as the sun sank west, wayfarers from all directions of the crossroads had come in to tarry over wine or ale. There were four men, burly and loud, still coated with soot from the mines to the south, and one family from Tessyry to the west — man, wife, son, and daughter. The children chased each other in figure eights around the legs of the table they all sat at. In the northwest corner, three men in the grey robes of The Temple sat, bearing faces made of stone as grey as their robes.

Agwen was busy serving food and drink to the tables and making sure mugs were full. Detmar, arms crossed, sat on a stool by the door, his face hidden by the storm cloud of his beard. Cal went over to him and subtly nodded toward the table of templemen.

"Do they come often?"

"No idea if they did when it was Aggie's aunt running it, but they seemed pretty interested in coming after we arrived. We were visited by that Seoran, the tall one with the snub nose, the previous day. Why? Any heresies from you we should know about?"

Cal's thumb ran along the strings of his fiddle. "No. But busybodies who speak to the gods always make me nervous. You're never too sure if they actually do or just think so."

Detmar made a motion with his broad shoulders that suggested mountains collapsing. "We'll find out soon enough when you play if they're looking to burn you at the stake. You can have a drink before playing. See Aggie now that she's back at the bar."

When Cal turned, he saw the two children looking at him. The boy sat in his mother's lap, arms outreached, babbling incoherencies that conveyed the level of want he had for Cal's motley. The girl held on to one table leg, gazing with wide eyes at the colors of Cal's outfit with one thumb in her mouth to placate herself.

Cal decided to caper instead of walk to the bar. Indulging in a shambling spindly gait caused giggles to break out at the family's table, and cheers and laughter from the miners. Cal liked that the cheers were not jeers, the laughter not tainted with mockery. Even the templemen just fixed him with a collection of stares that seemed less disapproving and more guarded curiosity. By the time he reached the bar, Agwen had already poured out a mug of ale, so dark he could see only a shadowy reflection of his face where the layer of creamy foam had split open. He took one strong sip then looked at Agwen, who met his gaze with a cocked eyebrow.

"Would you mind starting early? Perhaps finish the first set with a lullaby, so the family can head upstairs for bed and leave a table for any stragglers for the second or third?"

Cal nodded, went to a space in the center of the room, and waited with the bow held in the air and fiddle tucked under his chin. The conversation did not take long to die down to mere murmurs. With that, he began to stomp out the rhythm with his boot's heel.

He knew they expected him to launch into a local drinking song like "For All I Have Is This Mug." Instead, going through the vast recesses of his memory, he fished out and played for them something from the east, from the Isle of Aire, "A Warning For Your Thirst."

Cal tilted his head to watch the puzzlement on people's faces give way to smiles as they listened, and began to appreciate the intricate wordplay he spat in between bursts of music he played from the fiddle. He glanced at the Tessyry family. The mother was leading the children to clap along with his foot's beat. The stern-looking father remained stone-faced, but Cal could see one dirty fingernail tap the table along with the rhythmic clapping of the children. Cal knew they could be relied on for the rest of the set.

He glanced over to the table of miners, blinking as it seemed the light had become a bit dimmer. He could still make out the diverse range of their faces. Some were likely raised and born here, some farther afield from seaside towns like himself, and one, clearly from the western isles, a smile already on his face. Likely a Sommari. That determined Cal's next song.

He gave them no warning, speeding up his stomping foot's pace and moving the bow down the bridge. He saw the miners' expectant looks, then, when he burst out a phrase in the Sommari tongue, with an explosion of laughter, they pointed to their Sommari friend, whose smile switched to open-mouthed astonishment. He would have to return in a song or two to give the local miners a tune to call their own, but for now, he had them.

He blinked again. It definitely seemed like the inn was getting darker, but decided not to wait for Detmar to light another lantern. Another night, he would wait for the second or third set to concentrate on the templemen, but since he had conquered the two other tables so quickly, he felt confident this table of unsmiling acolytes would soon succumb to his musical charms.

As his second song finished, Cal forsook his usual pattern and instead relied on silence and his bow's flourish, as he turned towards the templemen's table. He figured one of their hymns reworked into a jaunty jig would win them over, but Seoran, the tall snub-nosed man the other acolytes deferred to, looked resistant to even his charms.

Knowing what he had to sing, Cal launched into a less morose version of a melody familiar to those acolytes. However, he did not use the language of today when he sang, but instead showed off how it was a hymn in the Elder Tongue, from the days when the kings and queens of long-vanished Santona ruled over the lands he now traveled through.

He blinked again, realizing the templemen's faces had grown more concerned than pleased. Slightly thrown off, his delivery of the following lines of supplication was hoarser than he liked. One of them, a youth to the left of the snub-nosed leader, pointed a finger at him.

No… pointed slightly to his right. At the fiddle he still had tucked under his chin.

He improvised a quick run with his bow across the bridge, then pulled away from the fiddle with a flourish and glanced at his instrument.

His strings were glowing. A pale luminescent glow.

His foot still kept the rhythm, so, biting his lip, he tucked the fiddle back onto his shoulder and started up the melody again. Whatever was happening, he needed to see more.

He glanced around. All of his audience kept their attention rapt upon him. It seemed only he and the templemen shared the secret of the glow.

As he sang the second refrain in the Elder Tongue, Cal saw what he thought was grey haze hovering above the table lanterns gradually take shape. The haze, animated by faint sparks of light, spread into a human figure taking form, arms outreached to the templemen.

They, however, remained focused on him, till he stopped playing the fiddle and sang the final lamentation using just his voice's plaintive wail, unaccompanied by his foot's stomp and his instrument's music.

The two outstretched arms became encased in porcelain blue flesh. The indistinct shape in the center became a woman's, her face sorrowful and questioning as her eyes locked with those of the tall snub-nosed temple priest.

With a flash of flame, the table the templemen sat at turned over, casting their corner into darkness as the candle on it extinguished itself on the floor. The pale blue specter became better defined, so that everyone saw her.

Panic leapt from table to table. Detmar's heavy hand fell on Cal's shoulder and pulled him back to the bar as templemen, miners, and the family rushed for the door. Outside, horses neighed, hooves beat a tattoo, and wheels creaked as they all fled the Inn of the Seven Stars.

The glowing figure had disappeared. Glancing at his fiddle, Cal could see no more glow on the strings.

A sudden bang on the bar made him flinch. He saw two mugs of ale filled to the brim, as Agwen poured a third.

"Well, your show's over," she said. "Let's have a couple of drinks and figure out what to do next, shall we?"

Detmar grabbed a mug. Taking a swig, wiping away the foam it left on his upper lip with a sleeve, he spoke. "Well, now we know who or what's been leaving patterns in the dust overnight."

"You knew?" Cal asked in astonishment.

Agwen took a deep drink from her mug. "Not exactly. Strange sigils were being found in the dirt in the cellar every morning. It's what Detmar was digging holes for this afternoon. We were hoping for some bones. Much easier to figure out if a proper burial would have made it stop."

"Did you suspect your aunt of having done something?"

"It's not like we were close. But, honestly, if my aunt went the way of Mad Meladia and started killing her customers, I wouldn't blame her. It seemed like a good method to make money; have them stay and take them for all they're worth, bury them or feed them in a stew to the next unsuspecting customer. Seems much more profitable than running a nice little inn for people to lay off their worries for the night. Unfortunately, my husband frowns on cold-blooded murder."

"I'm sorry. But I told you as much when you agreed to marry me; that's on you, my dear," Detmar said, beard obscuring his mouth, but Cal suspected a smile hid underneath.

"So … so … you're not upset I summoned up a shade?"

Agwen laughed. "Of course we are! We were set for a good night tonight! I'll say this, everyone was having fun and ordering more ale than stew. You were doing great! Till the necromancy, of course. You should have told us you were a sorcerer. We would have politely sent you on your way."

"I'm not!" Cal glanced at his mug and realized it was nearly empty. "But the fiddle, the strings are encased in steel forged from the iron that fell from the stars over in Riftensberg. They're supposed to have mystical properties. Still. I assure you, a wizard I am not."

"I should hope so. Because if you were, I'd ask why you summoned up an ancient shade in front of some templemen to set us up to be run out of town, or worse."

"I'm sorry. Whatever happened there was not intentional. When I realized there was magic at work here, I had to play the song, though; it was the only way to know more. Do you know what this Seoran is like? This place seems far too away for them to summon up the Inquest."

Detmar nodded. "You're right. The temple priest will go for rousing the villagers to come at us, but from what we can tell, most people are relaxed. They are far from war and strife here, so their faith isn't their sole means of succor. Other than faith in a good day's work and good night's sleep." He walked over to the door and looked out in both directions. "It's too late in the evening. I say we have till tomorrow before we start getting visitors again."

Agwen tilted her head back to get the last drops from her mug. "Right then. If the templemen come in the cold light of day, we can say it was something in the stew, maybe blame it on that old grove we found in the forest in the back."

Cal felt the need to speak up. "A grove?"

"Yes, very beautiful with shafts of light coming through the branches. Detmar and I went for a stroll, and the silence of the place was amazing. I nearly picked up some mushrooms growing out of an oak tree but Detmar thought they might be poisonous. Mind you, my husband has lived in cities and ships his entire life, and thinks carrots are also poisonous."

"Don't put words in my mouth. I said I'd rather eat poison than carrots, but the mushrooms could be poisonous."

"Were some of the mushrooms arranged in a circle, by any chance?" Cal interrupted.

Agwen nodded. "Why? You think that's where the ghost's body is really buried?"

"Not exactly, but the moon is not yet at its zenith. I think I might get some insight if you take me there, and with that, be able to get whatever mob comes for your blood tomorrow instead to forgive and forget."

"You know, for someone who says you're not a wizard, you sure act like one, what with the magic strings and now this."

"I'm no wizard, but I know a thing or two."

"Well, why are you staying to help us?"

"For the same reason you haven't killed me or run me out. You seem like good folk, and I'd like to play here if I come this way again."

"Detmar, clearly we have him fooled." Agwen said this with levity, but Cal noticed how Detmar reached out and grasped one of her hands that held longer than most.

He picked up his fiddle. "Detmar, can you show me the way?"

"Wait." Agwen took his mug and refilled it. "You have time for one more."

•   •   •

Later that night, when a bashful moon, full and pale, hid behind passing clouds whenever they looked up, Cal and Detmar, both comforted by the warmth of the ale still within them, staggered with awkward grace into a grove some three hundred yards from the inn.

Detmar held up a lantern so that Cal could see the circle of toadstools to the left of the royal oak that held court over the grove.

As Cal expected, the circle was wide enough for a fully grown man to lie in.

"It's not that cold tonight, and we're not close on the calendar to any festivals of the dead who wish to come back. I'll be fine here, Detmar."

The lantern caused Detmar's eyes to be cast in deep shadows that showed the scars and lines of his mountainous face.

"If it weren't for fear of what might happen if I leave Agwen alone too long, I'd stand guard. It's what I was good at before I met her."

"Come back when the sun rises. I should still be here. If I wake early, I'll come back to the inn."

"And if you don't?"

"Tell anyone who comes I was an evil wizard who fled west. That might satisfy the templemen. If not, then I'm sorry for all this."

Detmar nodded, and Cal watched as the lantern shrank in the dark to a wavering star. drifting back to where the inn squatted by a road cut through this forest's heart for centuries.

Satisfied he was alone, and his eyes adjusted to the moonlight that silvered the glade, Cal looked at a sprout of three mushrooms that sprang in front of the oak. Plucking the central one, he went to the middle of the toadstool circle and gingerly sat down. He ate the mushroom he had plucked, then took his fiddle out of the satchel. Lying back in the grass, he cradled his fiddle like a newborn babe. His fingernails began to pluck out the first melody he had ever taught himself, before he even learned to use the bow. Humming the children's rhyme that went along with it, feeling a tingle in his cheeks intensify, he closed his eyes to dream.

After some time, a pressure on his chest caused him to open his eyes. He did not see the moon shining through a web of jagged branches. Instead, he beheld at cathedral arches of built-up golden mist. A silvery mist, reminiscent of the pale glow that had affected his fiddle strings, lurked just outside the fragile undulating barriers.

A voice that sounded like a choir of insects sang unto him. "Forgive the rather sparse settings. We have not had a visitor in quite a while."

Cal looked to his left and saw the mist thicken and condense into something like a stone fireplace. A fire, casting the same ghostly light as what surrounded him, lit up within, and he felt surprising waves of heat from it.

Standing in front of it was a tall, slender figure of feminine beauty stylized into caricature. Winged ears sprang out from a cascade of blood-red hair, framing a narrow-pointed face. Gossamer wings fanned out from the figure's back, twitching slightly.

Cal tried to speak, but the pressure remained on his chest, vibrating with a rumble. Still feeling as if in a dream, he realized the weight on his chest was a grey cat with claws fastened in his motley jerkin.

"Don't mind him." The winged figure tittered. "A child buried his corpse in my grove a century ago. The mushroom you plucked springs from his grave, which attracted his attention. He was buried here, the girl hoping I could bestow a resurrection on her childhood friend, not realizing she would live longer than he could ever possibly do. I could not, but I let him come and go as he pleases in this realm. Still, I gather you would prefer to sit up for a conversation."

At a clap of her hands, the grey cat jumped off Cal's chest with a loud miaow, and then sauntered away into the mist.

Finally sitting up, Cal took a couple of breaths before speaking. "I am Calmondo, one of the new men, who comes to you to seek knowledge of what has transpired in these woods."

He saw lips pull back in a smile, while black orbs for eyes reflected the light from the fire.

"Considering the history I have seen of you mortals, I have more than enough to tell you. I could tell you of the empires that have risen and fallen, several times, until you wither to dust. Is that what you want?"

"As flattering as it would be to spend the rest of my life giving you a moment's diversion, I am afraid I seek a specific bit of knowledge."

His words were chosen well, as she laughed a sound both musical and unnerving to listen to.

"What then, Calmondo, do you seek?"

"There is a woman who lived during the time of the kingdom of Santona. It was an era you'd know, when sorcerer-kings allied with your folk. Her shade haunts where the roads crossed, and there is a longing within her that keeps her tethered."

"Ah. There has been a recent fluttering of activity in that direction. It's been silent for spirits until very recently. I feel the threshold was crossed as of this night. Have you been committing necromancy, oh mortal Calmondo?"

"Not exactly; I am but a mere musician. Still, a song I played seemed to pull her through into this realm. Doing so thins the barriers between our worlds, and wherever the barrier thins —"

"Woe and misery take root. Yes, yes. A wizard once taught me the phrase from one of your poets when he came for knowledge. You mortals' bequests always amuse me. The ways to change the world are right there for you if you just pay attention. You say you're a mere musician. Do you really expect me to teach you some spells to cast this shade begone?"

"Perhaps as a favor, you could take a more direct hand."

The figure laughed again, but Cal did not like the mocking undertone, even if it reminded him of what exactly he was dealing with and to continue with caution.

"It is only because it has been too long since visits from your kind that I indulged an audience. My patience grows thin, mortal. Music was the key to unlock the door that held this shade back; so, too, must the key be the same to send her back to the grey realms and lock her away from returning. Write a song, a cycle of sonnets, to serenade her home. If you have the talent and the heart, you just might have the power to grant her the desire to return of her own volition."

Cal could not keep the bitterness out of his response. "If it was only that simple. My head is filled with scores, nay, hundreds of songs. Each one, I taught myself, to learn the ways of music, of how each one can evoke emotion in the listener to compel them to love, dance, and reflect on tender memories. Each time I try to make music on my own, I can only think of all the songs I know and where I am stealing the music from."

The figure gave him a quizzical cock of her head. The grey cat had wandered back in while Cal spoke and weaved itself around her legs, staring at him with emerald eyes.

"Then it sounds like you have all the songs you need to work the magic you seek. You just have to play them in the right order to give yourself the ending you desire, rather than the currently written one. The sun is coming up, mortal. Begone!"

She kissed his forehead, sending his skull aflame with pain.

Cal woke in the woods again, his clothes soaked with mildew, and the sky red with the promise of dawn.

He stood up, bones aching. He heard the trample of branches and saw Detmar's bear-like shape walking towards him. He waved his arm.

He knew what he had to do.

•   •   •

After a breakfast of ham and eggs and hot tea that helped him forget the taste of the mushroom consumed under the moon last night, Cal sat in a chair, plucking at his fiddle's string from time to time, not saying anything, as the two innkeepers arranged the place for new visitors.

He was lost in his thoughts when Detmar called from outside, where he had been standing as implacable as a great oak, gazing in all directions. He held an axe in one hand, and, as Cal came to the door, he pointed down the road.

Two score or more people marched towards them from the west, where the town of Laurent was located. A chant in the Elder Tongue came from among them. The templemen had had some success in rounding up the villagers this morning. Now the sun was high and shined down upon them all.

Agwen leaned out a moment later, sighing.

"Did the two of you want to stand out here to be easy targets for getting stoned alive or worse? Come inside."

As she went behind the bar, Cal stood near the cellar door. Detmar placed the axe on the bar top before easing himself on a stool, one hand resting on the haft.

As the chant grew louder, Cal winced at how out of tune the chanters were.

Yet, it gave him hope. It suggested more confusion and obligation than fear and rage.

The light through the door darkened as the tall snub-nosed temple priest stepped in, his face shrouded in suspicion. He focused his piercing gaze on Cal, who found himself at a loss of words when Agwen said, "Welcome, Seoran."

The priest looked over at Agwen, then realized Detmar was to his side, still and silent.

The moment grew thick with tension before the priest spoke.

"Let us not mince words. Your aunt had this inn before you, and while I could not detect any malice from her, I know she never accepted the faith of the Temple in her heart. Then you two come from far-off cities, bringing your ways here. I had not judged you. When you had what I thought was a minstrel here last night, I did not say anything, as it was not the time. However, sorcery is being harbored here, resurrecting shades of the dead. We would have merely questioned you, if you did not have the sorcerer right here, mocking us in his motley garb."

It was a speech conveyed with far more passion than Cal liked. It suggested that reason would not win today.

He tried to make out the shifting crowd behind the priest. Cal could feel their hesitancy despite the zeal expressed by the man who herded them here. He glanced at Agwen, who nodded, and he stood up and spoke with a loud but calm voice for the crowd to hear him.

"What happened last night was not through magic. It may have been a miracle sent by the gods."

The priest narrowed his eyes. "Are you saying you speak for the gods instead of us at the Temple?"

"No; it is the gods' choice to have one of their priestesses of the olden days bless us and bless this inn." He paused. "And to bless the people of the town of Laurent."

The priest burst into laughter. "Surely you are a wizard seeking to enchant us into accepting these lies."

"Why don't we let the people of Laurent decide for themselves?" Detmar said.

The priest glanced again in Detmar's direction, eyes widening when he noticed the axe on the countertop.

Cal knew they had a chance. The priest wanted the issue resolved, but likely doubted his memories of what had transpired. That doubt magnified within the crowd. Despite the old tales many had heard as children, the idea of an actual wizard coming to their town was undreamt of. Curiosity won out over fear.

"Good people of Laurent. You are more than welcome to come in and see for yourselves. I am but a mere musician. I will perform several songs to prove there is no wizardry at work here. Come see for yourself if the specter appears."

Agwen called out, "There's more than enough room. You are all welcome."

A weathered farmer was the first to step in, then the priest's acolytes, bearing questioning looks at their leader. Cal looked at the priest and saw he was biting his lip. The priest realized he had no real say in what the people would do. A burly smith, who looked like he could challenge Detmar at a wrestling match, and his diminutive wife followed. More farmers and young sunburnt fieldworkers approached. They all soon filled the Inn and took the seats Agwen had arranged in a semi-circle, a makeshift amphitheater for Cal's performance.

Cal knew what he had to do. But he also had no say in how the crowd would react.

He began as always with a rhythmic stomp of his boot. He set his bow to fiddle and launched into "March Towards Paradise." That song's widespread popularity had caused Cal's enthusiasm for the music to curdle over time. Still, at this moment, he needed the crowd to relax, understand his musicianship, let them gauge his voice, see he was no sorcerer of old but just a man like them.

The priest stood, reticent to the song's charms. Perhaps at another time, the priest and Cal would agree the simple platitudes expressed within were too treacly for either of their hearts, but now was not the time to talk.

He gave no break and let his bow move down the bridge, letting the chords deepen as he went into the next song, a tale of endless longing for love. Cal had learned it in the tongue of Fazhoul, but for now, he sang it in a rough translation. The original's subtleties would be lost, but the crowd needed to know the context.

Sweat trickled down his brow, but he refused to break playing to wipe it. He felt his face redden in the effort as he went through the third song, one of inviting strangers into your home that he had learned from a fiddler he had met on a remote archipelago to the north. The winters were dire there, emphasizing the song's exaltations of hospitality as a virtue.

Cal then began to have his vision darken, affected by his fiddle strings' newfound glow.

He glanced at his audience. So many faces, each a book of tales open for him to read.

He moved to a spiritual he had learned in an eastern seaport, an appreciation for the joys one had, of family and friends, of clear skies and full bellies, how all were accepted with gratitude.

Even with the day's light shining through the open door, he saw silvery ribbons form in the air.

It would be the next song, then the fifth, where he knew if it would work.

His playing slowed and grew sinuous. He sang of overwhelming desire, of how it could consume the soul till you opened your heart.

The ribbons coalesced into limbs, a column of a torso. Here in the daylight, it looked transparent, unreal, but as Cal heard the audience's murmurings, he did not perceive fear. He heard awe.

Now he moved back to where it all began. Cal sang the song that first summoned the shade, and in the Elder Tongue, details defined. The shade's beautiful face become apparent to all, with its expression of longing.

Now, he played one more song, at last, one of contentment he had learned from his journeys to the many-spired Zhanripul. He and the others saw the look of longing fade. Steadily, the shade's face softened into bliss.

The priest still stood, his mouth open with astonishment, but Cal could see the faraway look in his eyes.

The shade looked about them all. Silver hands bid them welcome, then gave a sign all people knew, since they were taught by the Temple, the sign that the gods wished them to carry in their hearts.

Be well.

The shade sank through the floor to where the cellar was. The glow soon faded from the fiddle's strings.

Silence reigned for a long moment, then the smith's wife was the first to applaud. Others joined in.

The priest did not, but he took a step back and nodded. There was no actual subterfuge of what they had witnessed, the emotions expressed. No charlatanry, and no malice either.

The inn was blessed, for it was on a holy site, and the people of Laurent were blessed to have it within a day's walk.

As the applause died out, the weathered farmer who first came in behind the priest raised his hand to catch Agwen's attention, his eyes shining with tears. His voice quavered as he spoke, "We are happy to have you here and keeping this inn open for all who come. May I trouble you for an ale in gratitude for allowing us this?"

And with that question, the tension broke. All who had arrived clamored for ale in celebration.

Though some left as the light grew dim, other travelers arrived, unaware of what had transpired the night before and the day just passed. Coming in were people filled with joy and contentment, lured by the sound of Cal's fiddle and voice. Soon strangers, too, became newfound friends in the Inn of the Seven Stars.

•   •   •

The following day, Cal woke up. His voice ached from the many songs he had sung, his fingers still tingling from all the playing he had done, and he suspected he was still lightheaded, as Agwen and Detmar had kept his mug full the entire night.

He took off his motley in favor of his traveling leathers. He packed everything away with great care to make no noise. Carrying his pair of boots in his hand, he crept barefoot down the stairs.

"Where do you think you're going?" Agwen said, as she and Detmar sat together eating their breakfast.

Across from them was a third chair with a bowl set before it and a small bag to the side.

"Come sit with us. The payment is here. You can count it if you wish."

Cal sat down with them, but shook his head. Between spoonfuls, he murmured, "That won't be necessary."

"You know, a musician who can work miracles could draw quite a crowd here," Detmar said, before pouring what was left of his own bowl down his throat.

"If a musician could always work miracles, perhaps. But you will not be troubled by that shade or any others now."

"Were you that good a player, who could summon the dead and send it back?" Agwen asked with a sly smile.

Cal leaned back in his chair.

"No. And do not ask me what her name was. But she was here when the Elder Tongue was spoken, and your statement of sigils found in the dirt below suggests she was a shrine keeper. I do not know if your aunt experienced anything, but her passing and the two of you arriving seemed to bring her back, or perhaps she was always here. When I sang a song in the language of her time, it awakened memories within her to come back. What I had to do was stir new emotions in her, emotions tied to memories that would allow her the peace to leave us for the grey realms again."

"So, you have no idea what she was here for?"

"That would require true necromancy. I am only a musician, but every song I sing is a means of conveying emotions. I can only think of the emotions that would be stirred within me and what I desire to feel. No matter where I travel, no matter what songs I sing, they are always about desire, and we are the same the world over for experiencing it."

"Do you feel you know all the songs of the world, then?"

"No. Until I am sent to my grave, I'm keen on learning new songs from corners of the world I have yet to set foot in, and new songs composed by new generations of people I meet as I cross lands I have been through before. Music is the one language we all speak. Whenever we experience music, it allows us to feel we are together. Whether living or dead." Cal slipped on his boots, stood up, and hoisted his satchel over his shoulder.

"You are always welcome back here, you know. We suspect we will be busy in the days or even years to come, but I'll have Detmar kick someone out of a room if we're full and you come this way again."

Cal nodded. "I make no promises when, but I will return if I can. You have my word."

"One final thing," Agwen said as she picked up their empty bowls. "That fifth song you played did not sound like any ballad or hymn I had heard before. Where did you learn it?"

Cal smiled. "It is a song of seduction taught in silk-clad chambers across the Southern Sea. I changed the phrasing somewhat, but the level of desire it expressed matched what the shade felt, and, I suspect, the priest as well."

"I thought that song sounded familiar," Detmar said, looking at his wife.

The two of them matched eyes, then laughed.

Cal gave a wordless farewell gesture as he left the Inn of the Seven Stars, letting the sun warm his face as he strode the well-worn paths, humming to himself one of the many songs he had fallen in love with in all his crossings of the world.

ABOUT THE AUTHOR

Kevin Beckett lives in a Canadian city that is on some nights colder than the planet Mars. At various points in life, he has been a radio show host, a nightclub DJ, and a music promoter, and he now runs social media & promotion for *New Edge Sword & Sorcery Magazine*. His previous works include "AKA The Sinner: Games of Dying Men" and "High Road to Hy-Brasil!" published in *Hell Hath No Fury* from Pro Se Press. He is working on more journeys with Fiddler Cal.

YOU MIGHT ALSO ENJOY

THE ALCHEMIST DAUGHTER
by Paul S. Moore

When a concoction of ethers channels a little of their magic properties to one location, inspiration springs to life.

GREY MOTHER MOUNTAIN
by Elyse Russell

When her village is destroyed, an elderly woman seeks help from the last remaining dragon to get revenge.

SONGS OF A DEAD FOREST
by Travis Wade Beaty

Old songs can bring new life.

Available in digital and trade paperback editions from
Water Dragon Publishing
waterdragonpublishing.com

9 781959 804567